Shake Before Opening

Shake Before Opening

Jez Alborough

RED FOX

For Line

A Red Fox Book

Published by Random House Children's Books
20 Vauxhall Bridge Road, London SW1V 2SA

A division of Random House UK Ltd

London Melbourne Sydney Auckland
Johannesburg and agencies throughout the world

First published by Hutchinson Children's Books 1991
This edition Red Fox 1992

Copyright © Jez Alborough 1991

The right of Jez Alborough to be identified as the
author of this work has been asserted by him in
accordance with the Copyright, Designs and Patents
Act, 1988.

Printed and bound in Great Britain by
Cox & Wyman Ltd, Reading, Berkshire

ISBN 0 09 992640 7

Contents

Hall of Mirrors

Only 50p to   come in   and look round

Chattering Teeth

I've got a toy —
some chattering teeth
with feet that patter underneath.
I often sit
and wonder why
they remind me of my Auntie Vi!

No Limits

I know a boy whose party trick
is athletical arithmetic.
He boasts a strange ability
to count up to infinity.
Incredibly, this feat he reckons
will take him less than fifteen seconds.

He draws quite large for all to see,
the symbol for infinity.
Then drops his head askew, askance,
gives the sign a sideways glance
and then proceeds to demonstrate
by counting quickly
up to eight.

The Human Pulse

A camel
is a mammal,
and so's
a wolverine.
A frog is an
amphibian,
and I'm
a human bean.

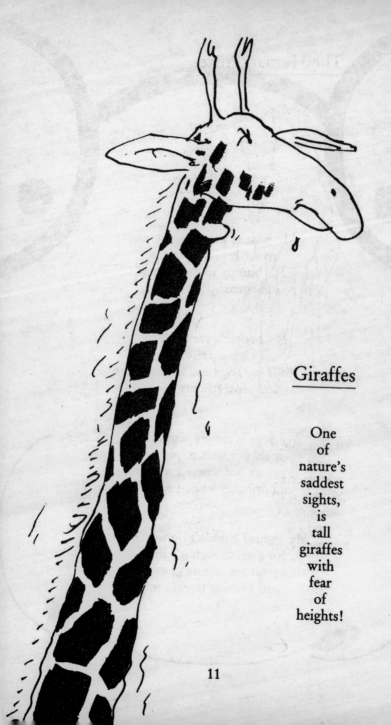

Giraffes

One
of
nature's
saddest
sights,
is
tall
giraffes
with
fear
of
heights!

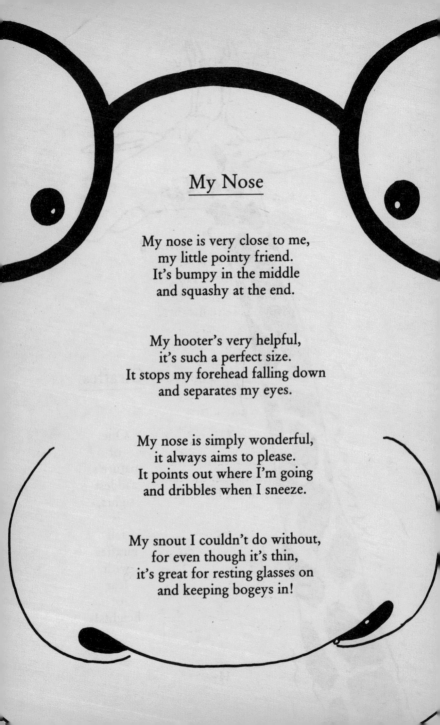

My Nose

My nose is very close to me,
my little pointy friend.
It's bumpy in the middle
and squashy at the end.

My hooter's very helpful,
it's such a perfect size.
It stops my forehead falling down
and separates my eyes.

My nose is simply wonderful,
it always aims to please.
It points out where I'm going
and dribbles when I sneeze.

My snout I couldn't do without,
for even though it's thin,
it's great for resting glasses on
and keeping bogeys in!

Ear Popping

To blow your ears clear
hold your nose.
And with a POP
the blockage goes.
But please remember,
pay regard.
Never blow too long
or hard.
I knew a boy
who didn't stop
when at first
he heard no POP.
He blew until
his face turned red
and POPPED the ears
clear off his head!

School Time

We've got
a crooked clock in class.
Its seconds take
an hour to pass.
Except at playtimes!
Then it's bound
to be the other way around.

Now

Don't ask me why,
don't ask me how,
this moment that we know as **now**
will very soon be passing, when
it won't be **now**
but will be **then**.
And stranger still
when **now** is **then**
it quickly changes back again.
Don't ask me why
Don't ask me how
But even when it's **then**, it's **now**!

SUMmary

No satisfaction in subtraction.
No ambition with addition,
No precision with division.
I'll never be a mathematician.

Fourteen Fingers

I've fourteen fingers
    want to see?
Fourteen fingers
    stuck on me.

Fourteen fingers?
No you never.
Show me then
if you're so clever.

Watch my hands,
I'll prove to you
that what I say
is really true:

Two fourfingers . . . that makes eight.

Plus two times three —

That's fourteen mate!

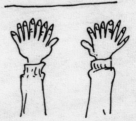

17

Counting on You

You cannot count
to more than five
on four fingers and a thumb.
But, on the other hand . . .

of course, it can be done!

The Palm Reader

Examination
Turn the page
Concentration
Brains engage
Clock ticks slowly
Minds move quick
Questions, questions
Tick, tock, tick.
Someone here
is taking chances
watching out for
teacher's glances.
He tells the future,
knows he'll pass.
There's always one
in every class.
He hides inside
a crooked arm
and reads the answers
on his palm.

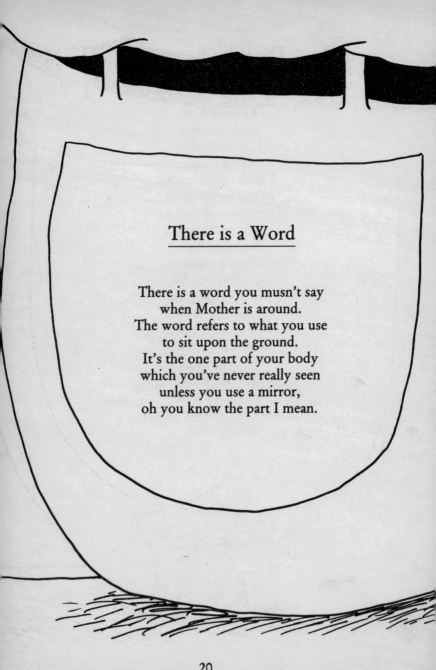

There is a Word

There is a word you musn't say
when Mother is around.
The word refers to what you use
to sit upon the ground.
It's the one part of your body
which you've never really seen
unless you use a mirror,
oh you know the part I mean.

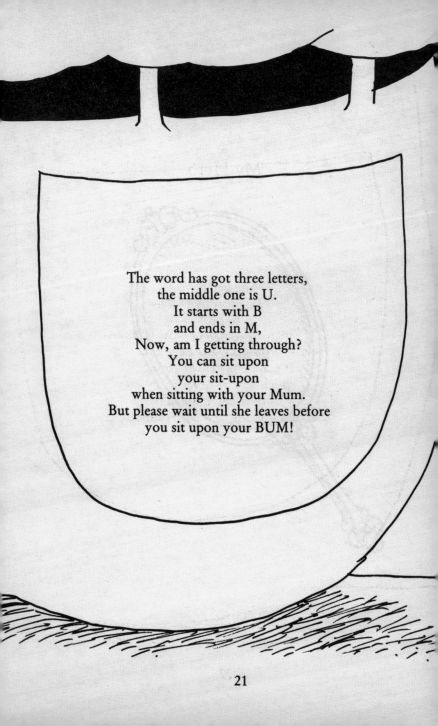

The word has got three letters,
the middle one is U.
It starts with B
and ends in M,
Now, am I getting through?
You can sit upon
your sit-upon
when sitting with your Mum.
But please wait until she leaves before
you sit upon your BUM!

My Hero

The person
I'd most like
to be
is someone
by the name of
ME!

Growth

All over his chin
and under his nose,
right down his legs,
on top of his toes.

All up his arms
(and under them too)
even the back of his neck has a few.

Growing on shoulders
and over his back,
some short and some curly,
some grey and some black.

My Dad is so hairy
he belongs in the zoo.
I hope when I'm older
that I will be too!

A Hot

The central heating in my head
has turned my cheeks tomato red.
I'm burning up, my throat is dry,
my thermostat's been on too high.
No sneeze or wheeze or runny nose,
no shivers, quivers, none of those.
It's not a cold I've gone and got,
I've gone and got myself a hot!

Green Knees

Short trousers.
Green knees.

Green →

Skidding footballer disease.

Pierce with a Straw

Don't stir
Pierce with a straw.
Keep cool.
Tear off along
dotted line.

Dead Ant Stew

I'm not much good at cooking
but there's one dish I can do.
I make it in a bucket
and I call it 'Dead Ant Stew'.

I mix up water, mud and grass
and nettles that I pick,
then squish ants dead and drop them in
and stir it with a stick.

If you want to try this dish,
take heed the final bit . . .
before you serve it up make sure
you top it off with spit.

The Invasion

They journey here on special boats,
from hot and distant countries.
They travel to our shops in vans
and hang around in bunches.

They bend like ageing grannies but
they're only inches tall.
Their flesh is soft and squashy
with no bones inside at all.

Their skins are dry and yellow
and their freckles come out black.
They come from distant countries
but we never send them back.

You meet these creatures all the time
yet never are you flustered.
You simply chop them into bits
and eat them up with custard.

Going in the Sea

I'm in the sea,
I need to pee,
but there's something
stopping me.

Though there is
no toilet near,
it seems all wrong
to do it here.

It feels so naughty
to pursue it,
what if someone
saw me do it?

The colour of it
wouldn't match,
I'm sure I'd leave
a yellow patch.

And what about
the sea's pollution?
It doesn't need
my contribution.

My bladder won't
accept the notion,
it's just a piddle
in the ocean.

Imagine how
the sea would be
if everybody
went like me!

I know it's wrong,
I know, I know,
but now I've simply
GOT to go.

There's no more time
for being shy.
If fish can do it . . .
so can I!

First Day at the Big School

New boy
out of place.
Short trousers,
long face.

The Kiss Thief

Don't flap and fuss
whatever you do
if Simon steals a kiss from you.
Don't tell the teachers,
Don't complain . . .

or he might give it back again.

Chatter Box

We all possess a voice box,
my teacher said we did.
The trouble is some people never
want to close the lid.

The End of Summer Holidays

Winter whistles,
Rain drip-drops,
Seven weeks of playtime stops.
How could summer be so cruel
to end and send us
back to school?

Big Brother

Two years stronger,
faster,
taller.
Two years
more EVERYTHING
than me.
Two years younger,
slower,
smaller.
Two years less
I'll always be.

Three years slower,
smaller,
shorter.
Three years
less everything
than me.
I'm glad I've got
a little sister . . .

Three years younger-er than me.

Courage

I come unarmed with sandwiches
inside a plastic tub.
I don't rely on Mummy
to provide me with my grub.
I like to live with danger,
you can see it in my eye.
I'm a school dinner kind of person
not a 'packed lunch' sort of guy!

Dinner Ladies

Where do dinner ladies eat
while you enjoy their cooking?
They pop out to the burger bar
when no one else is looking.

Cold-weather Friend

With pleasure written on your face
you hold him in a warm embrace.

But when his warmth has gone, instead

you coldly kick him out of bed.

A Tissue

A . . . tissue. Ah . . . ahh . . . tissue

I need a . . . Ahh AHH . . . AHHHH . . .

AAHTISHOOOOO!

I thank you!

Walking the Plank

I say I do.
He says you don't.
I say I will.
He says you won't!
He says prove it!
I say no!
He says see . . .
I told you so!

I say *you* do it.
He says I might.
I say let's see you then.
He says all right.
I say you couldn't.
He says I *could*.
I say you wouldn't.
He says I *would* . . .
I would
if I wanted,
but I don't
and here's why:
You chose not to do it,
so why shouldn't I?

Don't Lean Back on Your Chair, Claire

Don't lean back on your chair, Claire.
Don't lean back on your chair.
Don't lean back on your chair, Claire.
DON'T LEAN BACK ON YOUR . . .

I'm the Captain

I'm the Captain.
No you ain't.
Yes I am. What's your complaint?
You always are.
Ain't it strange!
I'll be the Captain for a change.
Oh yeah!
Yeah!
Well, tell me, Billy,
whose ball is this?
It's your ball, silly!
Exactly, so just shut your mouth
'cos *you* don't have a say.
It's my ball
I'm the Captain.
And, who said you could play?

In a Spin

I spun around,
I whirled and twirled,
and with me spun
a blurry world.
But when I stopped
and hit the ground,
the world kept spinning
round and round.
The world is meant to spin, I know,
but only really, really slow.

Crikey! Blimey! Help! Disaster!
I've made the planet spin much faster.
What will all the people do?
They'll have to speed *their* pace up too.
And when they walk along the street
they'll feel it race beneath their feet.
The world will be one fast and mean
giant exercise machine.

Everyone will soon be parted
from where they were
before it started.
Unless, like me, they hit the ground
and hold on while it's spinning round.
My dad is going to have a fit
when he finds out I started it.

But, just a minute, hocus-pocus,
the world is coming back in focus.
There's people walking, no stampede,
it's slowing down to normal speed.
Disaster struck the world and yet
the people don't look too upset.
Incredible, what I begun —
with such a simple spin I spun

Keep in a Cool Place

The temperature is greater
nearer the equator.
Pity the poor souls
who freeze around the poles.

Perspiration

Salty water
from within.
Symptom of
a leaky skin.

Nature's Party Trick

A yawn is nature's party trick
to make you feel embarrassed quick.
It gets you in a public place,
then starts to rearrange your face.

Your mouth is forced to open wide,
revealing everything inside.
And when you try
and shut the hole,
you find your mouth
has lost control.
And while it gapes,
a yawn enjoys
making a gruesome
moaning noise.
And there you stand,
a howling beast,
for what feels like
an hour at least.

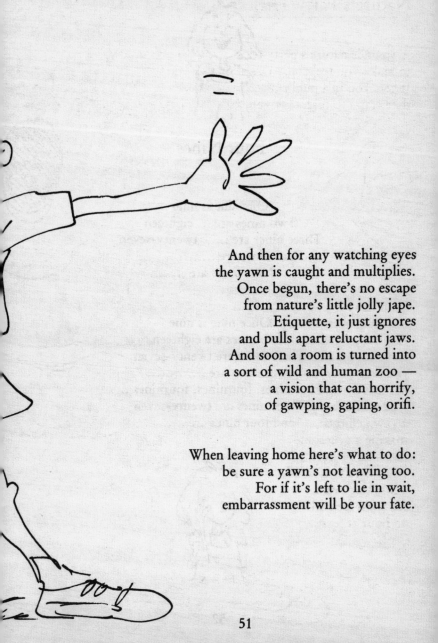

And then for any watching eyes
the yawn is caught and multiplies.
Once begun, there's no escape
from nature's little jolly jape.
Etiquette, it just ignores
and pulls apart reluctant jaws.
And soon a room is turned into
a sort of wild and human zoo —
a vision that can horrify,
of gawping, gaping, orifi.

When leaving home here's what to do:
be sure a yawn's not leaving too.
For if it's left to lie in wait,
embarrassment will be your fate.

Four Nines

One nine is nine
Two nines are ... eighteen
Three nines are ...... twenty-seven
Four nines are ....
... Nine fours are ....

Once nine is nine
Two nines are eighteen
Three nines are twenty-seven
Four nines are ....
Four nines, fournines, fournines ...
Three nines are twenty-seven
and four nines are ....

Twenty-seven
Twenny-eight
Twenny-nine, thirty
Thirdy-one
Thirdy-two
Thirdy-three
Thirdy-four
Thirdy-five
Thirdy-SIX
FOUR NINES ARE THIRTY-SIX
Definitely!

I think!

The Statue

His memory will be preserved
to stand the test of time;
frozen into history,
a soldier in his prime.
He stood upon the battlefield
and helped our country win,
now he's standing in the park
beside a rubbish bin.

He doesn't bat an eyelid,
his anger never shows
when children climb all over him
and scribble round his toes.
He holds up high his lofty head
so pigeons can alight,
but knows that as the years go by
his hair is turning white!

The **,** and the Full **.**

A sentence deep within a book
was causing quite a stir.
Before its full **.** could be reached
a problem would occur.

Despite a **,** in between,
the readership would tend
to end up somewhat out of breath
before they reached the end.

Said the **,** to the full **.**
'All these words are packed too tight.
This sentence goes on far too long,
it isn't reading right.'

56

The full . bounced along the line,
inspecting every word.
'You're absolutely right,' he said,
'this passage is absurd!
The words will never disobey
the punctuation laws.
They know that I can make them stop,
while you just make them
pause.'

'We need more time,' the , said,
'but how can time be stolen?'
The full . hopped above his head
and made a ;

He stayed up there to chat a while;
the , found a friend.
The sentence read through perfectly,
at least until the end.

57

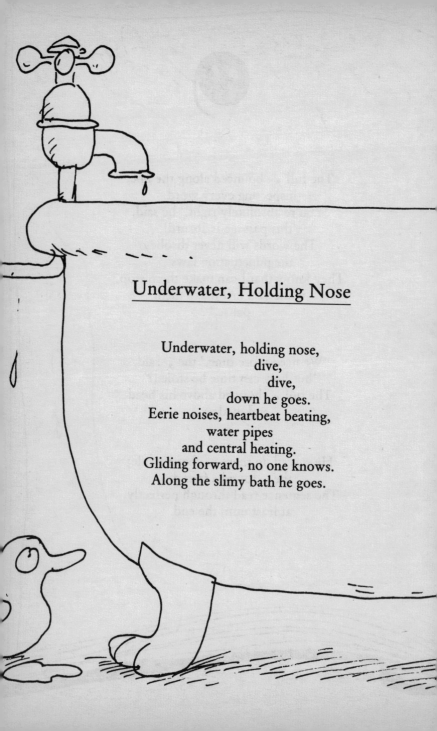

Underwater, Holding Nose

Underwater, holding nose,
    dive,
        dive,
           down he goes.
Eerie noises, heartbeat beating,
    water pipes
and central heating.
Gliding forward, no one knows.
Along the slimy bath he goes.

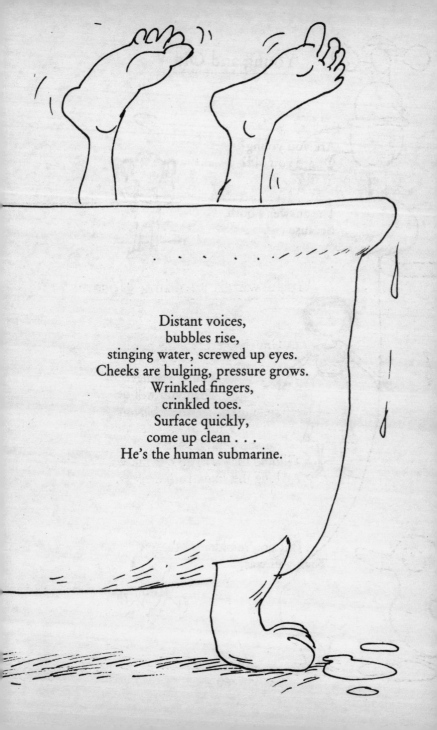

Distant voices,
bubbles rise,
stinging water, screwed up eyes.
Cheeks are bulging, pressure grows.
Wrinkled fingers,
crinkled toes.
Surface quickly,
come up clean . . .
He's the human submarine.

Young and Old

Are you young?
Or are you old?

The answer's both
Because . . .

You're younger
Than you will be. . .

. . . But you're older
Than you was.

Dead Inaccurate

A lifetime's breaths
cannot be counted.
I knew a man who tried.
Just before the total came,
disaster struck . . .
He died.

The Magician

'Nothing up my sleeves,' he said,
as all magicians do.
But then he rolled his coat-sleeves up

and showed us it was true!

Where Does all the Darkness Go

Where does all
the darkness go
when morning
sheds its light?
It hides out
in Australia
and creeps back
in the night!

Mouth Music

Stop your brass.
Quell your strings.
Damp your horns
and squeaky things.

Shut your mouths,
PACK IT IN!
You're making such an awful din!

Heavy Rain

Heavy Rain
The forecast said.
I watched to see it fall.
One
Gigantic
Raindrop
Fell . . .

And squashed the Albert Hall!

Auntie OOOHS!

They oooh, they do . . . my aunties two,
each time they come to stay.
They look me up and down a bit,
then this is what they say:

'Ooh! hasn't he grown
Hasn't he grown!
My goodness gracious me
It seems like .... OOOH!
Just months ago..
He hardly reached
my knee.

Well, I never
Oooh! I say
He's shooting up so fast
He's put on... OOOH!
At least an inch
Since when we saw him last!

Ooh!
ooh

Ooh
Ooh

I find it so embarrassing.
I don't know what to do.
And every time they come around
there's more of me to OOOH!

If only there were magic pills
which worked in such a way
that inches which take years to grow
would sprout in just a day.

My aunties would be quite surprised
next time they came to stay.
They'd look me up and down in shock
and this is what they'd say:

They'd OOOH! for every inch I'd grew.
They'd be OOOHING! thick and fast.
But I'd for once enjoy those OOOHS!
'cos they would be their last!

Terrible at Football

I'm good at English, French and Maths,
my homework record shows it.
But I'm terrible at football skills
and everybody knows it.

I practise kicking all the time,
I really give my all.
But end up hitting air outside
instead of *in* the ball.

When the teams are picked to play,
I'm always left in line.
I will play in any team,
but who will play in mine?

Once, they *let* me play with them —
it seemed to make good sense —
for just by getting in the way
I'd help with their defence.

A long shot hit me on the head.
I heard our Captain scream.
The only time I'd touched the ball
I'd scored against our team!

I'm good at English, French and Maths,
my homework record shows it.
But I'm terrible at football skills
and everybody knows it!

The Baby-sitter

When Mum and Dad go out to play
with other dads and mums,
before they've even said goodbye
the Baby-sitter comes.

She doesn't seem to want to play
with older girls and boys.
She'd rather come and bother me
and play with all my toys.

I let her read my books and even
ride me on her back.
I have to keep this girl amused
till Mum and Dad get back.

I wouldn't mind this little job
if I were paid a fee,
but when the Baby-sitter leaves
it's *her* that's paid — not me!

Jennifer Dunbar
(Who's Always First to Answer)

OOH,  ooh . . .

Ooh, Miss . . . Please Miss
Me Miss Dee

I know it Miss!
Me Miss
Please Miss . . . Me.
Oh Miss, eeeh Miss
Meee Miss me
I know it Miss
Go on Miss
Please Miss Dee.

Yes, Jennifer?

Who, me Miss?
Yes Jennifer.
The answer Miss?
YES Jennifer!

Ooh Miss, it's err
I err . . . Oooh
It's err . . .
I err . . .
It's err . . .
What was the question
again, Miss?

Henry's History Homework

Dear Mr Morrisey,
I know you want a good excuse,
an' I'd give one
if I knew it.
But the only reason
it weren't done
was 'cos he didn't do it!

Henry's Mum

What a Goalhanger

He sweet-talks saved-up sweets off you
but never pays you back.
He borrows all your felt-tip pens
and uses up the black.

He copies last night's homework
and pretends it's just a lark,
And somehow always manages
to get the highest mark.

He pushes into dinner queues —
that nasty little runt.
He's always got a friend who's standing
right up near the front.

He's a sort of playground yuppy —
there's one in every class.
He hangs around life's goalposts
simply waiting for a pass.

Hector the Inspector

Honest Hector, our Bus Inspector,
was a walking lie detector.
No one ever rode for free
when on *his* bus, the fifteen B.
And if he found a cheat who tried,
he'd quickly terminate their ride.
For he believed it only fair
to pay the price to get somewhere.
And, sure enough, when Hector died,
he bought a ticket for the ride.
The bus he took was number seven
and on the front was written . . .
HEAVEN.

Running

What joy to run
without constraint,
not just to get
to where you ain't.
Neither to be fast
nor zappy,
but simply 'cos
your legs are happy.

A Smile

Smiling is infectious,
you catch it like the flu.
When someone smiled at me today
I started smiling too.

I passed around the corner
and someone saw my grin.
When he smiled, I realised
I'd passed it on to him.

I thought about my smile and then
I realised its worth.
A single smile like mine could travel
right around the earth.

If you feel a smile begin
don't leave it undetected.
Let's start an epidemic quick
and get the world infected.